Penelope Popper

Book Doctor

Toni Buzzeo

Illustrations by
Jana Christy

UpstartBooks

Madison, Wisconsin
www.upstartbooks.com

To two of the best: Shonda in the library and Steve in the classroom.
—T. B.

To Harry and Hugo, for letting me continue to read to you, even though you're taller than me. I love you.
—J. C.

Published by UpstartBooks
4810 Forest Run Road
Madison, Wisconsin 53704
1-800-448-4887

Text © 2011 by Toni Buzzeo
Illustrations © 2011 by Jana Christy

The paper used in this publication meets the minimum requirements of American National Standard for Information Science — Permanence of Paper for Printed Library Material. ANSI/NISO Z39.48.

Penelope Popper wanted to be a doctor.
She had a doctor coat. She had a doctor bag.
She even had a doctor badge.

Penelope practiced doctoring as often as possible. But not everyone liked Penelope listening for heartbeats,

taking blood pressures,

and checking reflexes.

Even her teacher, Mr. Hempel, was often too busy for a check-up.

One Friday afternoon, Penelope was awfully discouraged.

"Go visit Ms. Brisco in the library, Penelope," Mr. Hempel suggested. "Maybe she can help."

Penelope packed up her doctor bag and headed down to the library.

"Any new doctor books?" she asked.

"I'm sorry, not today," Ms. Brisco said.

"Well, then, how's your heartbeat?" Penelope reached inside her doctor bag.

"Right as rain," Ms. Brisco said.

Penelope slumped to the floor.

"Why Penelope," Ms. Brisco said.
"Shall I take your blood pressure?"

"No." Penelope sighed.
"I just want to be a doctor."

"Which kind of doctor?"
Ms. Brisco asked.

Penelope gave her a puzzled look.

Ms. Brisco walked Penelope to the nonfiction shelves. "There are many kinds of doctors. People doctors. Animal doctors. And," she pulled a very old and tired book from the shelf, "book doctors!"

Penelope's eyes opened wide.
"What do THEY do?"

"I'll show you," Ms. Brisco said.

Penelope followed Ms. Brisco into a large back room. "Wow! What's all this?"

"Medical supplies." Ms. Brisco set to work repairing the dirty book and its torn pages.

When her patient looked almost new, Ms. Brisco slipped it into a Book Care bag. "THAT is what book doctors do!"

Penelope borrowed some art supplies from Ms. Brisco and stayed long enough to make a fancy sign for the back room door.

Book Hospital

Then she skipped back to class with the patient. "Look at this book!" she said.

But no one did.

On Monday morning, Penelope scanned the shelves and found three books that needed a book doctor's attention. She stacked the dirty books on the circulation desk.

"Penelope," Ms. Brisco said. "Would you like to be my medical resident?"

"What does a resident do?" Penelope asked.

"You'd learn to be a book doctor," Ms. Brisco said.

"Well, I have my doctor bag right here," Penelope said.

"Great." Ms. Brisco sorted through the pile. "Do you remember the first rule of book care?"

"Wash your hands before reading a book," Penelope said.

"As you can see," Ms. Brisco said, "some children have forgotten the rule."

Take Good care of your Books!

In the Book Hospital, Ms. Brisco pulled a canister from the shelf and removed a damp wipe. "Books can get sick when they're dirty." She carefully cleaned the cover and spine of the patient.

"Cleaning wipes for books!" Penelope picked up the canister. "I can do that!" And she did.

Back in class, Penelope lugged the big classroom dictionary over to a table. She removed the canister from her doctor bag, pulled on her medical gloves, and set to work.

"What are you doing, Penelope?" Hunter asked.

"Practicing doctoring," she said mysteriously.

On Tuesday, Penelope handed Ms. Brisco two books, each with torn pages. "Book Care Rule Two: Turn pages from the upper right-hand corner," she said.

"Quite right." Ms. Brisco handed Penelope a roll of nearly invisible book repair tape. "Only a book doctor or resident can perform this operation."

Penelope watched Ms. Brisco demonstrate and chirped, "I can do that!" And she did.

Back in the classroom, Penelope laid the big classroom dictionary open on the table.

"Please give Penelope room to perform this delicate procedure," Mr. Hempel said.

Penelope gently smoothed the torn page and matched up the torn edges until the letters on the page lined up perfectly. Then she carefully attached a strip of book repair tape on each side of the page.

"Hey," said Jada. "It's like when the emergency room doctor stitched my forehead back together!"

"Book Care Rule Three: Never dog-ear a page," Penelope recited before school on Wednesday morning. "Use a bookmark instead."

"Precisely." Ms. Brisco set Penelope to work making a big stack of Book Care bookmarks. "Thanks for helping me spread the word. Dog-eared pages are a real problem."

Penelope slipped the bookmarks into her doctor bag and settled down to browse through two books about veterinarians. She was shocked to find a dog-eared page in each. And one of the dog-ears was about to fall off!

She rushed to the Book Hospital and watched Ms. Brisco treat the first patient.

"I can do that!" Penelope said. And she did.

In Mr. Hempel's class, Penelope handed out the bookmarks to all of her classmates. "Meet me at the operating table and I'll show you why you need these."

She opened the dictionary to a dog-eared page and gently folded the corner back into place. Then she removed the backing from a corner-repair square. She carefully attached it to the page and smoothed it down.

Ruthie held up her finger. "It's like my splint."

On Thursday in the Book Hospital, Ms. Brisco handed Penelope a stack of plastic Book Care bags from the top shelf.

Penelope read, "Book Care Rule Four: Keep books safe from babies, pets and liquids."

"Unless students keep their books safe in these bags," Ms. Brisco said, "there's no hope for some books."

BOOK CARE RULES

1. Wash your hands before reading a book.

2. Turn pages from the upper right-hand corner.

3. Never dog-ear a page.

4. Keep books safe from babies, pets and liquids.

5. Use a shelf marker to hold your spot and then replace books carefully on the shelves.

Penelope glanced at the patient on the table. Its top and bottom corners had been chewed and its pages were rippled and stuck together.

"We can't save it?" Penelope cried.

Ms. Brisco shook her head. "We can only try to replace it."

Penelope handed out Book Care bags to each student in her class.

"What are you going to do to the dictionary today, Penelope?" Cameron asked.

But Penelope just shook her head sadly. "Just promise me you'll use the bags."

On Friday, Penelope discovered a book someone had shoved carelessly around another book on the shelf. The pages of the first book were bent and crumpled.

Penelope carried it carefully to the Book Hospital. "Someone forgot the last book care rule: Use a shelf marker to hold your spot and then replace books carefully on the shelves. Can we help?"

Ms. Brisco sighed. "Maybe." She smoothed the pages gently.

Penelope stepped forward. "I can do that!" And she did.

In the hallway, Sadie rushed up to Penelope. "Come quick!"

"What's wrong?" Penelope asked.

"It's the big dictionary," Sadie said. "It's fallen behind the radiator."

The book was wedged between the radiator and the wall, with its front cover bent back and many pages crumpled and folded.

Penelope reached deep into her bulging medical bag and removed her stethoscope. "What if we slide this under the patient and then lift very slowly?"

Mr. Hempel followed Penelope's instructions, and Penelope snatched the book into her arms. She rushed it over to the operating table.

Penelope cleaned the book with book care wipes. She healed torn pages. She smoothed crumpled pages back into proper position. Then she stretched two wide elastic bands tightly into place at the top and bottom of the book. "Now the patient will need to rest for a week."

When Penelope looked up, Mr. Hempel was standing behind the circle of classmates surrounding her. Ms. Brisco stood at his side.

Mr. Hempel cleared his throat. "Penelope, we have a gift for you."

He handed Penelope a small box. Inside was a shiny engraved badge.

Penelope grinned. "Will you pin it on me?"

Ms. Brisco removed Penelope's old DOCTOR badge and pinned on the new one. As she did, the class burst into applause.